# BAD BUNNY

Jonathan
Bentley

Scholastic Press • New York

Four little bunnies
lived together in the woods.
They hopped and skipped and frolicked,
just as all good bunnies should.
But wait! The fourth is missing!
Wherever could he be?

Here he is! The other one they like to call . . . **BAD BUNNY!**

He likes spicy sauce on everything
from donuts to ice cream.

Then he sneaks it on the vegetables
to make the others SCREAM!

These bunnies keep so nice and clean,
so soft and very fluffy.

Bad Bunny likes to bathe in slime!

He's stinky and he's scruffy.

Good bunnies like to dance and prance
and smell the scented roses.

Bad Bunny likes to stomp around
and TOOT right up their noses!

Danger came into the wood
on one fine sunny day.
The bunnies fled when they all saw
Sly Fox had come to play.

He chased them round and round,
as he drooled and chomped and snapped.

He spied Bad Bunny and he thought,
*What a tasty bunny snack!*

Bad Bunny saw him coming
as a plan formed in his head.
He stood up tall and brave,
then he cleared his voice and said,

"Before you eat my friends
and I in one big foxy bite,
would you like to try a donut?
It's a sugary delight!"

"Why, thank you," said the hungry fox,
"I'll make it my first course."
He swallowed it down whole,
not expecting . . .

Sly Fox turned fiery red,
then he scampered far away.
Though Bad Bunny was very naughty,
he had saved the day.
All the other bunnies cheered,
"He's saved us from that brute!"

Bad Bunny smiled and then
he made a very special . . .

For M, H, and R—J.B.

Originally published in 2022 by Scholastic Australia, an imprint of Scholastic Australia Pty Limited.

Library of Congress Cataloging-in-Publication Data available

ISBN 978-1-338-89759-3

10 9 8 7 6 5 4 3 2          23 24 25 26 27

Printed in China 179

This edition first printing, July 2023